A pucking good Christmas

DL GALLIE

Copyright © DL Gallie 2022

A Pucking Good Christmas

First published in the **Our First Christmas** anthology, 8 November 2022

Published independently 1 December 2023

Email: dlgallieauthor@outlook.com

Edited by **Karen Hrdlicka**, Barren Acres Editing
Cover Designed by **Kristie,** Vanilla Lily
Proofread by **Lisa Edwards**
Formatting and interior design by **DL Gallie**

'Tis the pucking season.

Kallen finally has the girl and they're about to celebrate their first Christmas as a married couple. And Chelsea has a present for Kallen he'll never forget.

However, when his rivalry with Stefan Däuchmen spills over from the ice into their personal lives, it threatens to not only melt their careers but Chelsea's surprise for her husband too.

KALLEN

... early October

WITH MY EYES STILL CLOSED, A SMILE APPEARS on my face as I register what's happening beneath the covers. My wife—fuck, Chelsea is now my wife—currently has her lips wrapped around my dick, sucking me to the back of her throat. This is the best way to wake up on the first day of our honeymoon.

Lifting the sheet, I glance down to see my wife's beautiful hazel eyes staring back at me. She throws me a wink and then focuses on the task at hand. Her head bobs up and down as she sucks on my shaft, the tip hitting the back of her throat, causing her to gag a little. Call me a dirty asshole, but that sound has my cock hardening further. She cups my balls and presses on THAT spot close to my no-go zone and from the evil glint in her eyes, she did that on purpose. "You'll pay for that," I hiss, which turns into a moan when she rakes her teeth gently along my length.

My cock slips from her mouth and she shakes her head. "No go for you. No go for me." Then she swallows my dick again and all thoughts about the no-go zone evaporate as I focus on the pleasure my wife is currently sucking from me. *How the puck did I get so lucky to score a wife like this woman?*

Gripping my cock at the base, she squeezes as she sucks the head. It doesn't take long before my balls begin to twitch. "Do it," she mumbles around my shaft and as if my body is in sync with her words, the first spurt shoots into her mouth. She sucks and swallows every last drop before my cock pops out of her mouth. She wipes at the corner and sucks her finger into her mouth. I know I just came but seeing her do that has my dick sparking back to life.

Beckoning to her with my index finger, Chels snakes her way up my body, dropping kisses along the way. She straddles my chest and stares down at me. "You beckoned, husband?"

"I did." I nod. "I want you to come up here and sit on my face. Once you've come on my tongue, I'm going to fuck you hard and fast from behind and then make sweet, sweet love to you for the rest of the day."

"As you wish." She lifts herself and hovers above my face, giving me an unobstructed view of her dripping pussy.

"Did that turn you on, baby? You're dripping."

"Maybe, but less talking, more licking."

"As you wish." I grip her hips and slide her to my mouth. Licking her from taint to clit, she moans when I circle my tongue over the sensitive bundle of nerves at the top. She lifts her hands and plays with her tits as I suckle on her clit.

"More," she demands, and I know exactly what she wants. Sliding my tongue down her slit, I thrust it inside her, flicking it around before sucking. She swivels her hips and rides my tongue and face. Gazing up at her, her eyes are closed and she's giving herself over to the pleasure building. Her arousal is dripping down my chin, she's never been this wet before. I could drown in her juices and I'd die a happy fucking man.

"Kal," she cries, "I'm ... I'm coming." Just as she says this, a torrent of her arousal soaks my face. I lap at her pussy like a starved man as she rides out her orgasm.

She leans forward and rests her head on the headboard, panting and still sitting on my face. "That," she pants, "was amazing."

"Mmmhmpf," I reply against her pussy. She giggles at the vibrations and lifts herself off my face and collapses to the mattress beside me. Looking over to her, I find her staring back at me with a blissful grin on her face.

"Good morning."

"Good morning, indeed." Rolling to my side, I lean over and press my lips to hers. What starts out slow, quickly turns heated. "Pussy and penis breath kisses are the best."

"You're disgusting," she mumbles against my lips.

"You love me."

"I'm questioning my love right about now."

"Too late, we have a piece of paper that says, 'til death do us part and you, Mrs. Jones, are not dying until I've had my fill of you."

"And how long will that be?"

"For at least fifty years. Minimum. But in all honesty, no amount of time will ever be enough with you."

"Kal, that's beautiful."

"You know what else is beautiful?"

"What?"

"This." I roll on top of her and my cock easily slides inside her and we make sweet, sweet love together. I know I said I'd fuck her hard and fast from behind first, but we have our whole lives for that to happen AND it's only day one of our honeymoon. I still have four uninterrupted days with her before we have to get back to New York to continue preseason training.

I'm lucky my coach also happens to be my wife's dad and he gave me a few days off to get married and for us to have a quick honeymoon. We could have waited until the next off-season to get married, but I couldn't wait another minute to be married to this amazing woman. So, four months to the day I proposed, we became man and wife.

Marrying Chels was the best day of my life, even better than the day I was drafted to the Crushers. Hockey won't be forever but what Chelsea and I have, it will last till the end of time, and even then, it won't be enough.

2
CHELSEA

... late October

THE NEW HOCKEY SEASON IS UNDERWAY AND THE
Crushers are currently at the top of the leader board.
I love watching hockey but I hate it when the
Crushers play the LA Legends because my ex,
Stefan Däuchmen—affectionately nicknamed
Doucheman because well, he's a douche and lives up
to the douche in his name—plays dirty, on and off the
ice, especially when it comes to my husband.

You'd think he'd have given up on his grudge
now that we're married, but nope, he's still a douche
with a capital D. It's not as volatile but it's no picnic
in Central Park either, and I think that's due to his

handler, Wren Brooks. Yep, Stefan now has a babysitter. Wren was hired by the LA Legends management and board to keep him in line and work on his image. She seems like the nicest girl ever, and I feel sorry for her having to babysit him.

On the ice, Stefan is an amazing player but off the ice, well, he's not so amazing. For the most part, since she started working with him, he's kept himself in line on and off the ice, but once a douche always a douche. I really hope they're paying her big, super-huge bucks because I have no doubt she's working twenty-four seven, three hundred and sixty-five days of the year keeping his douchey ass in line. I bet she's thankful that leap years only happen once every four years, and we just had one. Hopefully, by the time the next one comes around, she will be free of the douche and his antics.

We are in the final period and there are two minutes left on the clock and these two minutes are turning into the longest two minutes of my life. My heart is racing. My palms are sweaty and I feel like I'm going to throw up, again. This game is intense.

There's only one minute remaining and the score is tied, three to three. Doucheman has the puck and he's headed straight for Kal in the net. The rest of the Crushers seem off in la-la land because Doucheman easily makes his way through them. Weaving in and out of them, the only one who's trying to stop him is JJ.

We're now down to twenty-six seconds left in the game and it's all going to come down to this shot. Everyone in the stadium is on the edge of their seat. The atmosphere is electric and my heart is beating so fast, I'm expecting it to beat through my rib cage and land at my feet. "Come on, baby, you've got this," I chant to myself over and over. I'm now rocking back and forth in my seat watching Doucheman skate closer and closer to the net, and Kal.

He raises his stick and swings, executing a perfect slap shot. I jump to my feet and watch the puck sail through the air. Kal reaches out just as the siren blares and there's a collective gasp from those around me.

"Where's the puck?" someone from next to me asks. Just as they finish their question, Kal opens his glove and the puck falls to the ice, he saved it. They will now go into overtime.

The Crushers fans go crazy, as does the rest of the team on the ice. They all skate up to Kal and slap him on the back and helmet, while Doucheman stands there in shock that the puck was stopped. From the look on his face, he's pissed. No doubt

Wren will be scrambling to stop him from going into douche mode as soon as the game is over.

Five minutes later, they take the ice again and Doucheman is out for blood. He's returned to the ice like a raging bull with a red flag waving in his face. He's body checking left, right, and center, determined to not let the Crushers score. He's just Kronwalled JJ into the plexiglass and has the puck, he makes a breakaway and is headed for the goal and Kallen.

Once again it all comes down to Kallen against Stefan.

Like the last period, my eyes are locked on him as he makes his way down the ice. He really is a great athlete, it's just a shame about his personality and persona. Kal is watching him intently, much like I'm watching them.

Stefan is flying down the ice, he's got some speed behind him, rather than launching into another slap shot, he heads straight for Kal and the goal. He's going for a wraparound this time and skates to the right, knowing that Kal's left isn't as good as his right. He circles the back of the net and with a flick of the wrist, hits the puck, and it sails past Kal into the net.

The Legends win.

"Puck," I mumble to myself as I jump up from

my seat and quickly make my way into the belly of the stadium to wait for Kal. He's going to be devastated. Losses always suck but when he loses to Stefan, it's always harder to take.

It feels like it's taking him forever to come out. His teammate, JJ, and Lexi, the team's physical therapist and now JJ's girl, exit first. "How is he?" I ask, pushing off the wall to walk over to them.

"I think you know how he is," he replies. His face confirms what I thought, Kal is pissed at himself for the loss.

"Puck," I mumble, just as a wave of nausea rolls over me. Racing over to the nearest trash can, I empty the contents of my stomach. This bug is just lingering, every time I think I'm better, it strikes again.

"You okay, Chels?" Lexi asks me, running her hand over my back.

"Yeah, that bug I picked up in Cleveland last week is still hanging on. Add in the nerves of the game just now, and well, my nachos decided I needed to taste what they're like on the way up. FYI, not as good coming up as going down."

"Duly noted, let me get you some water to wash away that nacho-flavored vomit."

"Thanks," I mumble as I wipe my mouth with the back of my hand.

"I'll get it," JJ offers. I watch as he reenters the dressing room, leaving me to lean against the cinder block wall. Closing my eyes, I take a deep breath, willing myself not to barf again.

"Maybe you're pregnant," Lexi teases from beside me.

"Yeah, nah, it's just that bug. Dad was sick too if you remember."

"True," she agrees, "but you and your husband do bang a lot."

"I can't help it, have you seen my husband?"

"I have." She suggestively raises her eyebrows at me. "Your husband is H O double T, hot." And she's right, my husband is the hottest player in the NHL and he's all mine. There's no better feeling in the world than waking up beside him each and every morning. Actually, the best feeling is waking with his head between my legs and that magical tongue of his sliding through my folds before thrusting inside of me. Man, I wish I didn't feel like death warmed up, I could do with a tongue-induced orgasm right about now. I mean, it's been fourteen hours since his tongue was inside of me, that's forever in tongue time.

"Aww, thanks, babe," JJ coos, kissing Lex on the cheek as he hands me a bottle of water. "I think you're H O double T, sexy as fuck too."

"Thanks, but for the record, you're only H O T hot, no double T for you," she teases him. He fakes being hurt and then the two of them proceed to discuss JJ's hotness and the hotness ranking of each other.

Unscrewing the water bottle, I take a sip and watch the two of them bicker back and forth. I'm so glad the two of them pulled their fingers out and got over their issues. If two people are meant to be, it's those two.

Me throwing up again pulls them apart, and just like last time, Lexi rubs my back while my body expels the water I just drank.

"Chels, babe," Kallen voices, rushing over to me. "Are you okay?"

"I'm fine," I tell him. Wiping my mouth on the back of my hand, I turn to face him and smile. "That bug from Cleveland is still hanging on and kicking my ass, but YAY, I didn't vomit during the game."

"That's good, hope it's not anything more serious."

"Maybe she's—" JJ's sentence is cut off when Lexi covers his mouth with her hand.

"... going to be okay," Lexi says. "I was thinking I'd take her home and you two can meet us there after you wrap things up here." She pauses. "Maybe also go and have a few drinks with the boys, let Chels and I have some girl time."

"Thanks, Lex, I appreciate you looking after Chels like that, but as her husband, I should be looking after her."

"I'm not an invalid," I add, "I can get from the stadium to home by myself."

"I know, babe, but I just worry about you."

"And I'm fine," I sneer, hoping he can't tell I want to vomit again.

"Chels, throwing up in the trash can twice isn't fine," JJ states. "To appease us, please let Lex look after you and I'll look after your man."

"I'm—"

"Please, babe," Kal says, pulling me into his arms. He slides his around my waist and I drape mine over his shoulders. "For me?"

"Fine," I relent.

"Thank you." He places a kiss on the tip of my nose. "Now go home and warm the bed up for me. Then when I get home, we can—"

"LALALALALLALALALA," JJ singsongs,

putting his fingers in his ears. "I don't need to hear about you two bumping uglies."

"Why?" Kal asks. "We all heard you and Lex in her treatment room yesterday before training."

Lexi's eyes widen and her cheeks darken in embarrassment, meanwhile, JJ grins like the guy who scored ... and technically he did. "What can I say? My lady is—" Once again, Lexi covers his mouth.

"Do not finish that sentence, James Jameson ..."

"Ohhhhhhh, you just got full named, you're in trouble now," Kallen teases and I smack him in the stomach. "What?"

"Be nice, otherwise, there will be no ..." But before I can finish that sentence, I throw up again.

"Doesn't look like you'll be getting any tonight, Jones," JJ teases him.

"And you won't be getting any either, Jameson," Lexi throws back at him. "Come on, Chels, let's get you home."

"Thanks, Lex." I turn to Kal. "Play nice in the press conference and then enjoy your night with the guys."

"You sure?"

Nodding, I smile and reach up to cup his cheek. "Very sure. Now go and get your drink on."

"Love you." He leans in for a kiss, but I cover his mouth with my hand and shake my head.

"I have nacho-flavored vomit breath and before you say anything, that's worse than morning or pussy breath, so don't even try to argue with me."

"Fine," he hisses against my palm. "But tomorrow, when you're feeling better, I'm going to kiss your pussy and then share a pussy breath morning kiss with you before we spend naked Sunday together. And FYI, I might kiss your pussy several more times with both my mouth and my dick."

"What is it with you and my hoo-ha?"

"I'm addicted. One taste and I was hooked."

"Lucky I love you, Jones."

"That I am. And for the record, I love that you love me, Mrs. Jones." It's still surreal to be called Mrs. Jones but I wouldn't have it any other way. We've only been married for a few weeks now, but it's perfect in every way.

"Let's go, Jones," JJ yells as he's joined by Jett and Cliff from the team.

Kal kisses me on the cheek and then walks off with the guys. Lexi links her arm with mine and we watch them head toward the press conference. When they're out of earshot, Lexi leans into me. "First things first, we need to get a pregnancy test."

"I'm not pregnant," I snap.

"For me, please pee on a stick?"

"Fine," I relent, "but I'm not pregnant."

FYI ... I'm not pregnant, the test was negative. It's just a bug, like I keep telling everyone.

3
KALLEN

Leaving Chelsea with Lexi just now isn't sitting well with me, but I know my wife, when she's made up her mind, there's no changing it. Well, except for that one time I made her date me ... and then marry me, but that's all moot now. I slapped a ring on that and she's mine forever now. And one day, she'll carry my babies and we will live happily ever after.

"Dude, you okay?" JJ asks, slapping me on the back. "You were off in your head just now."

"Just worried about Chels."

"Dude, it's just a bug. She'll be fine."

"Yeah, I know but ..."

"But you love her and want to make sure she's okay, blah-blah-blah."

"You can't tell me if it was Lexi throwing up like that, that you'd be okay."

"Hell fucking no. I'd flip the team off and be there to hold her hair back while she vomits her guts up and then I'd feed her chicken soup and rub her feet."

"You're so whipped," I tease, bumping him in the shoulder.

"Like you're not?"

"Well, I'm here—"

"Only because she demanded you come here. See, whipped." He makes the sound of a whip cracking.

"Damn straight, I am. Have you seen my wife?"

"I'm not falling for that again, last time I agreed with you, you whacked me in the leg and I could hardly walk for a week."

"And I stand by that whack. No one ogles my wife except for me."

"And the millions of people who see the two of you on Page Six every time one of you sneezes. If it isn't baby watch, it's saying that her and Doucheman are sneaking around behind your back."

"Hell will freeze over before that ever happens."

JJ laughs at me but it's true. Chelsea will never go back to him and it's not just because she's with me, but because he broke her trust and her heart.

"Speaking of hot, have you seen his babysitter? She's H O double T hot and what adds to her hotness? The way she stands up to and handles Doucheman."

"Yeah, seeing her all feisty and in his face does things to me that I shouldn't be feeling." Everyone nods their heads in agreement over Wren Brooks. "And if Chels ever asks, I will deny this conversation ever occurred."

"Dude, none of us will ever admit that to our ladies. I don't know about you, but I like my balls where they are," JJ states.

"What, in Lexi's handbag?" Jett teases, causing us all to laugh.

"Fuck off, assholes." JJ flips us off and then cups his balls to reiterate the fact they are between his legs. "As you can see, my balls are firmly attached to my body."

"Physically yes, metaphorically speaking, they're currently at my place firmly in Lexi's grasp. Now that we know the location of your balls, can we stop talking about your balls?"

"I can't help it if you like my balls."

"I'd like to kick you in the balls right now."

"You wound me, Kal, you wound me."

"Fuck off, asshole."

We spend the next few hours at Squires drinking beer and ribbing each other at every turn.

When I finally make my way home, I find Chelsea sound asleep in our bed. Leaning against the doorframe, I stand here and watch her sleep. Her chest rises and falls with each breath she takes. I want nothing more than to crawl into bed and make sweet, sweet love to my wife, but I know she's not feeling well so I just stand here and watch over her.

She's so pucking beautiful, and I thank my lucky stars every day she gave me a chance. She swore never to fall for another player after Doucheman screwed her over but from the moment I laid my eyes on her, I was pucked. Unfortunately for her, I'm a persistent bastard and I wore her down. Now we're married and have the rest of our lives together.

"Are you watching me sleep again?" she mumbles.

"Yep," I reply.

"It's still creepy." She taps the mattress next to her.

Pushing off the doorframe, I walk over to her side

of the bed and sit on the edge. "How you doing, baby?"

"Feeling a little better now. Lexi thought I might be pregnant ..." My eyes widen and I'm pretty sure my heart stops.

"And?"

"I'm not, it's just a bug ... like I keep telling everyone."

"Ohh," I dejectedly reply. "For a minute there, I was excited you might have been." Pulling back the blanket, I cover her stomach with my hand. "I can't wait for the day your stomach swells with the baby we created together growing inside of you."

"I am too, but for now, I want to be selfish and have you all to myself." She raises her eyebrows at me in that 'I want you to devour me' kind of way and it has me sitting here sporting a semi. One eyebrow movement and my cock's a goner for her.

"Are you sure you're up to it? A few hours ago you were vomiting in the trash cans at the stadium."

"That was a few hours ago. Right now, I feel fine and I really really want to practice making a baby with my sexy as puck husband." To reiterate she wants me to fuck her. She sits up and pulls her Crushers tee over her head, baring her gorgeous tits to me. Lifting her hands, she cups her boobs and with her middle fingers rubs her nipples. "But before we get to the baby-making, I want you to fuck my tits. I love feeling your dick slide between them."

"What my wife wants, my wife gets."

Quicker than *The Flash*, I strip out of my clothes and straddle my wife's chest. With my eyes locked on hers, I stroke my dick while she continues to play with her tits. "You ready, baby?"

"Always," she breathlessly pants.

Shuffling forward, I guide my cock to her tits and slide the head into the soft cushioning of her mounds. A moan slips free when her tongue glides over the tip of my shaft. Sliding it back, I push back through but this time, she lifts her head up and sucks on the head. "Fuck, babe. Your mouth and tits are phenomenal."

"Only for you, baby, now fuck my tits."

"As you wish." I throw her a wink and then I do as she requests. Undulating my hips back and forth, I fuck her tits. My shaft slides in and out and sooner than I would have liked, my balls begin to tingle. "I'm close," I grunt.

"Do it," she hisses and as if her words are the detonator, I come. Milky white streams splash across her tits and chin.

Wiping her chin, she sucks her finger into her mouth, and seeing her do that has my cock once again coming to life. "Really, already?"

Shrugging at her, I grip my shaft and stroke him back to hard. "What can I say, I'm an addict when it comes to fucking you. Now, remove your panties, it's your turn to come."

"As much as I'd love to, I'm spent and need sleep. Can we settle for a shower and a snuggle?"

"A sexy shower? A naked snuggle? Both?"

"With us, anything is possible, but right now I need a shower to rinse off the mess you made all over me."

Chelsea naked and wet, yes fucking please. Climbing off my wife, I offer her my hand. Pulling her up, I cup her face and slam my lips to hers. Pushing my tongue into her mouth, she wraps her arms around my neck and pulls me into her. Her cum-covered breasts press against my bare chest. My cock hardens further and when Chels whimpers into my mouth in that 'I need you to fuck me' kind of way, I know I'm going to get a sexy shower.

Unfortunately for me, it wasn't a sexy shower but I did get naked cuddles, and a naked Chelsea is better than nothing.

Blissfully happy, I drift off to sleep with my

naked wife's body wrapped around mine. The next morning though, I get a wake-up blow job, followed by a sexy shower and a full day in bed ... naked ... with my wife.

4

CHELSEA

... mid December

Lexi and I are sitting in Squires waiting for the guys to get here while Margot, my best friend and current drinks wench, heads to the bar to get a pitcher of beer. The guys played against LA earlier tonight and they kicked LA's ass. Like thrashed them, thirteen to zero. I think that's a history-making loss, better look that up because if so, that's a marketing dream come true. The promotion from that will be amazing. Doucheman was sent off in the last period for being, well, a douche. Poor Wren is going to have her hands full with him tonight. I remember what he was like when they'd lose when we were together. He's like a two-year-old throwing a tantrum after their balloon flies away.

Margot arrives with a pitcher of beer and I could kiss her, my throat is dry and I'm thirsty as hell. "I ordered wings too."

"Awesome, I'm famished," I tell them as I pick up the pitcher and begin to pour us each a glass.

"How are you famished?" Margot asks me as she takes a seat across from me. "At the game you ate an order of nachos, half of Lexi's, three hotdogs, and two giant pretzels."

"What can I say, I'm a growing girl."

"Yeah, outward," she teases. I was about to hand her a beer so I stick my tongue out and hand it to Lexi instead.

"Maybe you're pregnant," Lexi adds from beside me and thanks me for her beer. A sense of déjà vu washes over me, of her and I having this same conversation a few weeks ago but this time, I think she might be right. My boobs have been really sore the last couple of days, the nausea first thing in the morning is horrendous, and I'm hungry all the time. Like ravenous, I'll stab a bitch, hungry. My eyes widen and I flick my gaze between her and Margot, covering my mouth in shock.

"Nooooo, I'm not ... am I?" They both stare blankly at me. "Surely, not?"

"I don't know, are you?" she questions.

"I ... I don't know. I'd know if I was, right?"

"Well, when was your last period?"

"I don't know, I don't get one. I'm on that birth control that stops them to help with my endo."

"Babe, no contraception is one-hundred-percent effective," Margot unhelpfully adds.

"Abstinence is," I throw back at her.

"Yes," Lexi deadpans, "you and that hunk of a husband of yours refrain from sex all the time. NOT. Did I not catch you two in the locker room a few days ago?"

"Well, yeah, but I hadn't seen him all day."

"Case in point, right there, as to why you might be preggers, you two hump like it's an Olympic sport."

"So do you and JJ," I throw back at Lexi.

"We are talking about you right now." She points her finger at me. "You know, I'm surprised you don't already have a billion babies."

"Riiiight?" Margo unhelpfully agrees. "I've thought the same thing on many occasions."

"You two are crazy, let's reduce that number to three, three baby Kallens I can handle."

"Three billion," they both say at the same time, fist bumping before falling into a fit of giggles while I continue to freak out that I may in fact be pregnant.

Lexi looks at me and when she sees me in freak-out mode, she sits up straight. "Look, Chels, I seriously think you'd know if you were, so have a great night tonight and let future Chelsea worry about it."

Nodding my head, I smile. "Yeah, you're right. I'd definitely know if I was, it's just my mind running rampant 'cause the heroine in my current read is pregnant."

"Exactly, now drink up." Margo lifts her beer and proceeds to chug it back. Shaking my head, I sit back in my chair and lift my drink to my lips but for some reason, I don't take a sip. I stare into the bubbly amber liquid and internally freak-out. Lexi and Margo start discussing a girls' trip away but I can't focus, I just keep thinking about the fact I might be pregnant.

I'm not, am I? Sure, Kal and I hump like rabbits but we're newlyweds and he travels for work. Surely not.

Before I fall into full-blown panic mode, the guys arrive. My husband sweeps me off my chair and into his arms before he smashes his lips to mine. For a few brief seconds, I stop my internal panicking and focus on the man currently squeezing the life out of me. Then I quickly push away, what if I'm pregnant? He'll squish the baby if he squeezes me like that.

"You all right, babe?" he questions, worry etched on his beautiful face.

"Yeah, I'm fine, I just need the bathroom." Looking to the girls, I shout louder than necessary, "Bathroom. Now."

They both look at me with confusion but they sense the silent pleading/impending freak-out I'm spiraling into because they both jump up and drag me out of my chair. We loop arms and the three of us walk away from the guys toward the restrooms.

When the guys are out of earshot, l whisper-hiss, "I think we need to get me a pregnancy test."

"Come again?" Margot questions when I flip the lock on the main bathroom door. Sorry, ladies who need to pee, but I need one-on-one noninterrupted freak-out time with my girls.

"I ... I think I'm pregnant." They both stare at me wide-eyed and open-mouthed. I've left Margo speechless, something I've only managed to achieve a few times in our life.

"With a baby?" she finally asks.

"No with a pucking gorilla, of course a baby."

"We were only teasing you." She adds, "You don't have to get so momma-bear."

"I know but ..." I shrug and subconsciously cover

my stomach with my hand and begin to gently rub circles.

"Holy puckballs, you really think you are, don't you?" she squeals when she realizes I really think I am.

Nodding, I stare at my two bestest friends and smile. "I ... I really think I am. My boobs are sore. I feel sick all the time—"

"And earlier today you ate as much as Kallen and JJ combined."

"I didn't eat that much." They both give me the 'really' look. "Okay, fine, I did overeat a little but forget about that, what am I going to do?"

"I can duck out to a pharmacy and get you a test," Margot offers as she takes my hand in hers, squeezing in that reassuring best friend kind of way, letting me know it's all going to be okay.

I shake my head from side to side. "I'm not taking a pregnancy test in a bar's bathroom."

"Well, how about we head home early?" Lex suggests.

"No." I shake my head again, but this time the action causes a lump to form in the back of my throat, and I feel like I want to vomit. "I can't duck out, I need to be here to celebrate tonight's pucking amazing win."

"But what if you ARE pregnant?" Lexi asks me, she looks worried that I'm considering waiting to find out.

"I'll still be pregnant tomorrow, Lex. Tonight, I'll play wife and tomorrow Chelsea can play the 'what if I'm pregnant' card."

We all nod in agreement and when we open the door to the restroom, we come face to face with Wren. She looks on the verge of tears but before we can see if she's okay, she darts past us into the restroom. Then we hear a frustrated growl from a deep voice at the end of the corridor. Hearing that makes me really want to check on her and make sure she's okay but before I have to make a decision, the door opens behind us.

Spinning around, I come face-to-face with Wren. She smiles at us and mumbles, "Excuse me." Lowering her head, she shuffles past us only for an arm to reach out, grab her, spin her into the wall of the corridor, and their muscular body cocoons her in.

My eyes widen and then I take off toward them, just as I hear her sneer, "Back the fuck up, Stefan." She presses her hands into his chest but he doesn't move, even though the tone of her voice means business. Stopping mid-stride, I stare at them when I realize who she's fighting with. I really don't want to intrude so I stand here and watch them. I'm once again shocked when I hear Stefan utter two words that I never thought I would hear him utter, much less to a woman. The words "I'm sorry" just passed through his lips. What the actual fuck? Stefan Däuchmen just apologized.

From beside me, Margot grabs my upper arm and digs her fingers in and whisper-hisses, "Did ... did Doucheman just apologize?"

"Mmmhmpf," I reply, nodding.

"What the actual fuck?" she sneers in shock. Her words cause both of them to snap their gazes toward us.

Offering a shy smile, I remove Margot's hand from my arm and take her hand. Dragging her and Lexi past them, I offer a small, "Excuse us" as we exit the restroom corridor. When we step back into the main bar area, Margot once again hisses, "What the actual fuck?"

A laugh breaks free. "You literally just said that, Margot."

"I know but, fuuuuck. Wren is a fucking miracle worker if she's getting him to utter the 'S' word."

"She sure is." I nod in agreement as the three of

us walk back to our table. All thoughts of me being pregnant vanish when I reach my husband, who is laughing with his friends and teammates.

6
KALLEN

"WHAT IS IT WITH CHICKS AND GOING TO THE bathroom in groups?" I ask JJ as I take the seat Chelsea just vacated.

"Beats me, maybe it's a safety in numbers thing."

"Who knows, but whatever the case, it's fucking weird."

"What's weird?" Jett asks, placing the two pitchers of beer he's carrying down on the table, while Cliff places the glasses down and the two of them proceed to pour beers for everyone, handing them out like the good beer wenches they are.

"How girls all go to the pisser together," JJ says.

"You really are crass sometimes," I tell him,

bumping his shoulder and causing him to spill his beer.

"Fucker, you made me spill my beer."

A commotion nearby snaps my attention and when I turn my head, I see Wren and Doucheman having a heated argument. "You really are a douche," Wren sneers at Stefan and from the look on his face, he's hurt by her words.

"And you're a stuck-up bitch who's riding my ass every five seconds."

"It's my job to ride your ass," she snaps at him. "Stefan, you're this close ..." She holds her fingers millimeters apart, "... to losing your career. To losing everything you've worked so hard for. I don't want to see everything go up in flames because you act like a Neanderthal, hot-headed dickwad."

"More like you don't want your reputation marred if I fail."

"Yes, I'm so shallow that I'm all about the 'look at me' crap. I'm not conceited like you. I actually fucking care." She turns and walks away from him. After a few steps, she spins back to him and gets up in his face. "You really are a self-centered, egotistical prick."

"And you're a sexy, uptight bitch."

They stand there, in the middle of the bar,

staring at one another. Each of them breathing heavily but the air has changed from heated anger to simmering with desire. Chels was right, there IS something going on between them, she'll be pissed she's peeing right now and missing this.

"Huh, didn't see that coming," I mumble, but clearly it was loud enough for them to hear because they both turn their heads toward me. Both stare matching angry daggers in my direction.

"Fuck off, Jones," Stefan snarls, "she's my handler. That's it."

Wren's head snaps back to him and there's hurt etched all over her face. She shakes her head and as she turns to leave, I notice tears welling in her eyes. Stefan stands there and watches her leave.

"Go after her, you fool," I shout at him.

"What?" he questions, confused at my words.

"For puck's sake, you two clearly have the hots for each other. Go. After. Her," I enunciate the last three words, spelling it out for him.

"Do not," he refutes, but his words are high-pitched and the tone used tells a different story. I see the moment the light bulb goes off in his head. "I—"

"Go," I tell him again and it sparks him into action. He turns and heads in the direction Wren raced off. He looks over his shoulder, indecision on his face. I nod in Wren's direction and then I sit here and watch as he goes after his girl.

A few minutes later Chels returns. "What'd I miss?" she asks, stopping in front of me.

"Babe, you will never believe it." Pulling her between my legs, I rest my hands on her hips. Placing a kiss on her forehead, I then fill her in on what we just witnessed.

"No pucking way," she says when I finish telling her. "That explains him saying 'I'm sorry' to her just now."

"Didn't know he knew those two words."

"Maybe Wren is perfect for him, professionally and personally," I say and then we rejoin the team to celebrate our massive win tonight.

It's nearing on close so we decide to call it a night. All us guys are well past tipsy but we're not yet shit-faced. The girls keep whispering like schoolgirls and my Spidey Sense is telling me that Chelsea is hiding something from me.

"Let's go home, husband," she declares, sliding her arm around my waist.

"Only if I get to fuck you in the as—" She covers my mouth with her hand and shakes her head from side to side.

"You know the answer to that, not happening ... ever ... unless I can—" Now it's my turn to cover her mouth with my hand. The cheeky minx winks at me and proceeds to lick my palm, circling her tongue over my skin. "I can do that to your dick," she mumbles against my palm.

"Taxi," I shout from behind her hand. This causes her to giggle and, fuck, I love that sound. Gripping her wrist, I remove her hand from my mouth. "Chels, we need to get home now before I take you into the bathroom and fuck you here."

My hand is still covering her mouth and she mumbles, "Taxi" just like I did.

Laughing, I bend down and throw her over my shoulder. Slapping her on the ass, I turn around and start toward the exit but I bump into someone and in my slightly inebriated state, the three of us fall to the floor. Chelsea grunts while a deep voice sneers, "Whats tzhe fusch asschole."

My eyes widen when I register that the voice belongs to a very drunk Doucheman and I mumble,

"Fuck," to myself as I offer my hand to Chels and pull her up.

"Wants a pieced of me, pricks?" he dribbles, clumsily pushing himself up into a standing position. Clearly he's had a few too many tonight. I look around for Wren but I can't see her anywhere. Looks like the two of them didn't kiss and make up after all. "You dids thatchs purpse."

"It was an accident," I snap back at the douche. "And you're drunk."

"Amsd snot," he throws back at me and then giggles. "Schnot," he repeats, chuckling to himself as if saying schnot is the funniest thing on earth.

"Where's Wren?" I ask. That was obviously the wrong thing to say because before I can process what's happening, his fist flies toward my face. I stumble backward from the hit and he comes at me again, causing the two of us to fall to the floor. He sucker punches me and my head bounces off the cement.

Someone pulls him off me and Chels drops down to see if I'm okay, but Doucheman gets free and knocks Chels to the side, trying to get to me. He stares down at me and I growl, "The fuck, man?" Jumping to my feet, I get up into his personal space, pissed off that he just pushed my wife. He's angry and drunk, his face red with anger and inebriation. Spittle forms at the corner of his lips and before I can say anything, he swings at me again.

"Ohh, it's on now," I growl through clenched teeth.

Curling my hand into a fist, I rear it back and slam it into his face. This pisses him off even more and he launches himself at me. The two of us crash into a high-top table before we roll and grapple on the ground. We go hit for hit and it isn't until someone separates us and shouts, "Break it up!" that we both stop.

Falling to my back, I breathe heavily, trying to catch my breath as I stare up at the ceiling of Squires. Rubbing my chin, I groan. I'm going to be bruised and sore tomorrow. I can't believe I just got into a fight with him, but the view and my internal processing is interrupted when an officer comes into my line of sight and hovers over me. "You're under arrest ..." *Ahh fuck, my wife and Coach are going to have my balls.*

7
CHELSEA

"Mom, this is all a mess," I cry as she slides a cup of coffee across the island counter to me. Dad is currently down at the police station, working on bailing Kallen out. Wrapping my hands around the mug, the warmth seeps into me but it does nothing to ease the anxiety coursing through me.

Bringing the mug to my lips, I take a sip and as soon as the liquid hits my tongue, I begin to gag. Placing the mug down, coffee sloshing everywhere, I race down the hallway to the guest bath and barely make it to the toilet before I throw up. Resting my arms on the seat, I continue to heave into the bowl.

A wet washcloth appears on my neck, followed

by the rub only a mom can do on my back. "That's nice," I murmur just before I throw up again.

Mom continues to rub my back and finally I stop vomiting. Closing my eyes, I rest my head on my arms. Not quite game to move just yet, that is until Mom asks, "How far along are you, honey?"

My head snaps up and I turn to face my mom. My mouth opens and closes a few times before I finally mumble, "I ... I ... I'm not pregnant." Wiping at my mouth with the back of my hand, I stare at her and smile. She returns the sentiment and offers me the washcloth for my face. "Thanks."

Taking the cloth from her, I wipe my face and hide behind the cool, wet cotton in my hand, avoiding Mom's stare.

"I think you might be pregnant, Chels," she says, and I know I have no choice but to face this now. She drops to the floor next to me and takes my hand in hers.

Removing the cloth from my face, I lean over and rest my head on her shoulder. She squeezes my hand in that Mom way and it immediately comforts me.

"How did you know?" I whisper.

"That reaction just now to coffee was exactly how I was when I found out I was pregnant with you."

"I ... I haven't done a test yet."

"Why not?"

"Because my husband got arrested for brawling in a bar with my ex-boyfriend."

"That's a good excuse."

"Mom," I plead, "what if I'm pregnant?"

"What if you are?" I nod absentmindedly at her words. "Surely you and Kallen have discussed children?"

"We have. We want three, but not for a few years yet."

"Well, when you have sex, pregnancy tends to happen."

"I'm on birth control," I defend.

"And no birth control is one-hundred-percent effective."

"Why do people keep reminding me of that?" Mom looks quizzically at me. "Margot said the same thing earlier tonight."

"Why didn't you test then?"

"I wasn't doing a pregnancy test in a bar's restroom."

"Fair enough." We fall silent but Mom breaks that a few moments later. "Okay, I'm going to run down the block to CVS and get you a test, no time like the present to see if I'm going to become a nanny."

Nodding, I sit here while Mom runs off to grab me a pregnancy test.

Twenty minutes later, Mom gently shakes me awake. "Sorry to wake you, honey, but A. You're asleep on the floor in the bathroom, and B. My neck hurt looking at you just now, and C. You have a test to take."

"Is it wrong that right now I'd rather do an algebra test than a pregnancy test?"

Mom laughs. "Chelsea Jones, I never thought I'd see the day you shy away from something."

"I'm not, I'm just ... scared."

"Welcome to motherhood. Not a day goes by that I don't worry about you."

"But—"

"Nope, no buts, you will understand when you become a mom. You worry constantly—"

"You make motherhood sound amazing," I deadpan.

"It's the most amazing job I have ever done. From the moment I saw that pink plus sign, I was in love. There hasn't been a moment since that day that I haven't thought about you. You are my greatest achievement, Chelsea, and I thank the puck gods every day for giving me you as a daughter. I love you baby girl."

"Mooom," I tearfully cry. "I love you too."

"I love you too, honey. Now that we know we love each other, it's time to pee on a stick."

KALLEN

It's lunchtime the following day and I've just made bail thanks to my coach and father-in-law, David. We climb into his car and the atmosphere is awkward, I can tell he's pissed off at me because I'm pissed at myself too. Brawling in a bar is not anything I've ever done before, but when it comes to Stefan Däuchmen I lose clearheaded thinking and I become a Neanderthal ... just like him.

Neither one of us utters a word as we pull out into traffic. The silence is deafening. I don't know what to say but what I do know is, right now, he's disappointed, frustrated, upset, and ashamed of me. I could go on with the descriptive words but of all the ones I've mentioned, it's the disappointing him part that is the worst thing about all of this. Actually, above all of that, not being there for my wife after she got shoved is the worst part, but disappointing Coach is a close second. I need to be a better husband and player, and right now, I don't know if he's angry at me in a son-in-law way or as my coach ... it's probably both, truth be told, which means I'm doubly screwed.

Fifteen minutes after leaving the precinct, we silently pull into the underground parking garage of my building, and I pull on my big boy panties and break the silence. "I know you're disappointed in me, you don't need to say it, Coach, I'm disappointed in me too."

"Wasn't going to say a thing," he nonchalantly replies from the driver's seat as he pulls into one of my guest parking spots, but his tone says it all. "But since you mentioned it, as your father-in-law, I'm pissed that you didn't look after my little girl. She's fine, by the way."

"I know she's fine, the arresting officer let me know."

"I expected this shit from *him*, not from you. You're better than that, Kallen."

"He started it," I snap like a petulant child. Like *him*.

"So mature of you, Kallen. Guess now's the time

to let you know that you've both been scratched for three games. You will each also be fined ten grand and at the upcoming Christmas charity day for underprivileged kids, you and Däuchmen will be required to give a talk on team bonding and how to deal with big personalities. Hopefully, doing this will prevent WWF matches between the two of you. Wren has arranged for both teams to be there as a buffer, we can't trust the two of you alone together. Coach Barber from the LA Legends and I feel it's time you two learn to play nice together."

"But—"

"No buts, Jones, this rivalry between you two has gotten out of hand. It's either this or indefinite suspension, I will not have the Crushers' name marred by you or him."

"Fine," I relent, "but I guarantee you, he won't be happy about this."

"I don't give a puck about him. I want you to man up and be the player and man I know you can be. Don't let Däuchmen and his antics bring you down. Kallen, you've worked too damn hard to let this rivalry dash your dreams."

"Fine." I huff, hating that he's right. I could lose it all if shit like this happens again. "You coming up?"

"Yep, Ness is upstairs, she stayed the night with

Chelsea. Wanted to make sure she was okay after being shoved, since you were otherwise indisposed."

"You just had to rub it in that I was a shit husband last night."

"No rubbing when it's the truth. Now get the fuck out of my car, you stink and you owe my daughter an apology. I hear she likes books with half-naked men on the cover."

Just like that, I know Coach and I will be fine. Now, I have to go upstairs and face my wife.

CHELSEA

The front door opens and in walk Kal and Dad. Jumping up from the sofa, I race over and throw myself at him. Thankfully, he has quick reflexes and he catches me as I wrap my legs around his waist and hug him for dear life. "Are you okay?"

"I'm fine, baby, but the question is, are you okay?"

"I'm fine," I tell him, but then I push on his chest and he lowers me back to my feet. He hugs me again and I gag, pushing myself away from him I cover my mouth. "Ugh, Kal," I mutter through my hand, "you stink."

"Told ya," Dad chortles as he walks over to Mom and envelops her in a hug. "How you doin', sweetness?" The two of them whisper together and then they start kissing, my parents are still so in love with each other it's sickening at times.

"Are you sure you're okay, baby? You took a pretty hard knock when Doucheman and I got into it." He cups my face and I cover his hand and smile up at him.

"I'm fine, Kal. No scratches or boo boos. Did you get everything sorted?"

"Well, I'm out," he dejectedly replies. He pulls me in for another hug and even though he smells like a dumpster, I hug him back. "I missed you last night," he whispers, kissing me on the head.

"I missed you too, please don't get arrested ever again. I was so worried."

"I'm sorry to have worried you, and I promise to never ever get arrested again."

"Good, so what happens now?" I ask him but before he can reply, Dad does on his behalf.

Turning to face him, I can tell from the stern look on his face, he's pissed off and I'm glad I'm not Kal right now. When Dad's pissed, it's not a pretty sight.

"Luckily for them both, no charges were pressed by Squires because Kallen and Stefan are going to head over there this afternoon and repair any damages themselves."

"That seems fair." I nod. "Anything else?"

"They both have been scratched for three games, each have been fined ten grand, and at the charity event next week, he and Däuchmen will be giving a talk on team bonding and how to deal with big personalities."

"Really, Dad? You couldn't go lenient on your son-in-law?"

Kal hugs me from behind. I snuggle back into him even if his stench right now is turning my stomach. I love being in his arms and I didn't realize how much I missed him until now.

"It's because he's my son-in-law that I imposed all that. I can't be seen as showing favoritism, besides this feud has been going on long enough. It's time to let bygones be bygones. What if you'd been seriously hurt, Pumpkin?"

"I'm fine, Dad," I argue with him, but when David Maxwell has made up his mind, there's no changing it.

"Your father's right, Chels, it could have been a lot worse for you," Mom interjects. I can see from the look on her face, she's referring to the fact that I'm pregnant and not that I'm a damsel in distress.

"I'm not made of glass," I snap, "and you both know that Kal would never let anything happen to me."

"I know, Pumpkin, but you're my baby girl. I will always worry about you." Dad pulls me from Kal's arms and wraps me in a hug. I stare over at Mom and I realize they're right, it could have ended badly for me ... and the baby. "When you become a parent, you'll understand."

My eyes widen when he says that. Does he know? Did Mom tell him? Pulling away, I look over to Mom. "Umm, Mom, can I get your help with something?"

"Sure, honey." She follows me down the hallway and as soon as I close the door, I whisper hiss, "Did you tell Dad?"

"No." She shakes her head. "I would never spoil your news but, honey, you need to tell him."

"I know I do, but what if he doesn't want kids yet? We've only been married a few months, it's too soon."

"There's no perfect time to have children, sweetheart. It happens when it happens, but you need to tell him."

"I know ... I think I want to wait. What if ..."

"Nope, no what-ifs. This baby is a fighter, he, or

she is a combination of Maxwell and Jones. Can't get any stronger than that. You need to share this with your husband. Your husband, who loves you to the moon and back, he'll be happy. Trust me."

Smiling, I nod and for the first time since I found out, I'm not freaking the puck out. "You're right, Mom, thank you." I pull her in for a hug. "I ... I think I want to give him the news as his Christmas present. Can you keep a secret for a little longer?"

"As much as I want to sing it from the rooftops that my baby is having a baby, I can wait, BUT please let me buy one baby thing for Christmas?"

"That's fine and thank you, Mom, you're going to make a fabulous granny—"

"No, I'm not Granny, I want them to can call me Nanny, Nanny Ness."

"And Dad can be Grumpy."

"I like that, but I think he'll be Grandpa ... just like his dad is Grandpa to you." She takes my hand and squeezes. "I'm so excited, Chels, but how are you going to gift this surprise to Kallen?"

"I have the perfect plan," I tell her with a smile. I just hope I can keep this secret for a little longer because I'm not very good with secrets.

KALLEN

"He's such a douchehole puckwit," I complain to JJ for the millionth time today.

"And you're acting like said douchehole puckwit." I eye him but he ignores me and tacks on, "Come on, man, you're better than this, and him. Three more hours and we're done."

"We still need to give our talk," I whine like a three-year-old who doesn't want to leave the park ... even though I'd be more than happy to leave right now. "How can I talk about being all buddy buddy with him when all I want to do is kick him in the nuts?"

"Fake it 'til you make it," JJ unhelpfully offers. "Look, you can either suck it up or face the wrath of

Coach, your wife, and an indefinite suspension. I know what choice I'd make."

"When did you become the levelheaded one?"

"About the same time I pulled my head out of my ass, manned up, and faced my feelings for Lex."

"Pussy-whipped," I snigger.

"Too right I am. Have you seen my sexy as sin girlfriend?"

Ignoring that question because we all know it's an opening for a punch, I go with a much safer question. "When you going to put a ring on that?"

"I've been thinking about it, but when's the right time?"

"When you know, you know," I truthfully tell him. I don't remember the exact moment I decided I wanted to marry Chels but as soon as the feeling hit, I had to do it. Hence why we had a short engagement, I didn't want her coming to her senses and changing her mind.

"That's not very helpful."

"Well, Christmas is coming up, an engagement ring would be a pretty amazing Christmas gift."

"Yeah, but then I puck myself over for future Christmases."

"New Year's?"

"Too cliche."

"Fuck, you're picky ... how about January third?"

"Why that date?"

"I just picked a date, you can't pick one so I did it for you."

"I kinda want to do it this year."

"Then December twenty-eighth?"

"But that date has no meaning."

"Puck me, JJ, you're so annoying. Just pick a date and slap a ring on it."

"I need to ask her dad first, but he's a scary dude and I'm kinda scared that he'll say no."

"If I can ask Coach for Chelsea's hand, you can ask Mr. Knight for Lexi's hand in marriage."

"Dr. Knight."

"Whatever, just man up, ask him, and then ask her ... on December twenty-first."

"I thought you said December twenty-eighth?"

"Pucking hell, just do it."

"Fine, I'll call Dr. Knight now."

"Good luck, but I'm sure the good doctor will be happy to give his blessing to the man who broke his little girl's heart before he finally grew a pair and swept her off her feet."

"You're a real piece of work sometimes, Jones. Go back to pucking Canada."

"I will, next month when we play the Vancouver Vikings."

He rolls his eyes at me, turns, and walks away with his phone to his ear. Like a creeper, I stand here and watch him, gradually sliding closer so I can hear him ask. I've never seen him look so nervous but after the question passes his lips, he holds his breath. He looks like he's gonna upchuck, glad I'm not in hurling distance, but suddenly he's smiling. I'm telling you, Ronald-freakin'-McDonald McSmiling. Clearly, Dr. Knight has given him the okay to marry his daughter. JJ offers me a thumbs-up, and I find myself smiling back at him.

"What's got you smiling like Ronald McDonald?" Chels asks me, sliding her arm around my waist and resting her head on my chest.

I chuckle to myself at her Ronald reference since I just used it myself. "JJ just asked Dr. Knight permission to ask Lexi to marry him and he gave his blessing."

"No pucking way."

"Yes, pucking way, and now you need to keep it a secret until December twenty-ninth?"

"Why not Christmas?"

"'Cause he doesn't want to ruin all the Christmases thereafter, hard to top a diamond ring for a gift."

"This is true, but why that date?"

"It's random and one I totally made up. I actually have no clue when he's going to do it."

"He needs to do it now 'cause I can't keep this secret." Looking up at my husband, I eye him. "Babe, you know I can't keep secrets."

"Even though you're keeping one from me now?" Her eyes widen and then it hits me, she IS keeping a secret. Pulling her closer, I stare into her eyes. "What are you keeping from me, Chelsea Jones?"

"Nothing, I'm—" She doesn't get a chance to finish her lie because we're interrupted by Wren and Doucheman.

"Sorry to interrupt," Wren says with a smile, "but Kallen, it's time for you guys to give your speech."

"Sure," I reply with a nod. Looking back at my secret-hiding wife, I place a kiss on the tip of her nose. "We'll finish this later," I tell Chels before I follow Wren and Doucheman to the front of the room.

We stand to the side of the makeshift stage and Wren begins explaining what's about to happen but I don't pay attention, I keep staring over at my wife.

Worry is etched on her face and that in turn makes me worry because she's hiding something. And as she said, she's the worst secret keeper in the history of secret keepers, so the fact that she IS hiding something means it's big.

"Focus, Jones," Doucheman growls at me. "I don't want you fucking this up for me, you've already nearly cost me everything, I won't have you do it again."

My face scrunches in confusion, what did I almost cost him? He's the one who got drunk and threw the first punch. He's the one who landed us in this predicament, not me. He's such a douche, but I don't have time to worry about that or my wife and her secret because, it's go time.

11
CHELSEA

Shit! Shit! Shit! I internally repeat as I stand here and watch Kal and Stefan follow Wren. He knows I'm keeping a secret and the hurt I saw in his eyes was a kick to the va-jay-jay. I know this secret will be worth the surprise, but maybe I need to tell him now. Christmas is still a week away and I don't know if I can keep lying to him like this. "Puck me!" I mumble.

Someone walks past me and heads toward the kitchen, the scent of raw meat hits me like a freight train and my stomach begins to churn. That 'ohh shit, I'm gonna vomit' lump forms in the back of my throat. "Be right back," I whisper to Lex and before she can say anything, I turn and race away from her toward the restrooms.

Just as I enter the restroom corridor, I hear her whisper-shout, "It's starting soon."

I make it as far as the family restroom and I know I won't make it to the ladies, so I slip inside. *Technically, I'm a family,* I think as I race over to the toilet. Dropping to my knees, I empty my stomach into the bowl. Whoever called it morning sickness has a pucking sick sense of humor because I feel sick all the pucking time. How Kal hasn't clued in yet is beyond me but then again, he has been preoccupied with today.

Dropping forward, I rest my head on the edge of the toilet seat and take a few deep breaths; in through my nose and out through my mouth. It works for a few fleeting moments but then the last of lunch decides to make an appearance.

Finally the wave passes and I push myself up. Walking over to the sink, I wash my hands and rinse my mouth. Drying my hands under the hand dryer, I spin and lean against the wall. Dropping my head back, I wipe my hands down my face. Keeping my face covered, I take another deep breath. Feeling somewhat human again, I swing open the door and step out into the hallway only to come face-to-face with Stefan. "Shit, Stefan," I pant, "I'm sorry, I didn't see you there."

"Are you okay, Chels?" He reaches out and rests his hand on my arm. That caring gesture reminds me of the man he once was.

Shaking my head, I quickly refute his claim and offer a smile, which I know isn't coming across as sincere. "I'm fine, Stefan."

"You look a little green, Chels. You sure you're okay?" I nod my reassurance again and then he tacks on, "For a minute there, I thought you might have had a bun in the oven."

My eyes widen and when he sees my reaction, his open too, mimicking mine. "Fuck me, you're pregnant?"

"Yes," I hiss, "but Kallen doesn't know and you can't tell him. Don't be a douche and ruin my Christmas surprise."

"You are the worst secret keeper ever. How does he not know?"

"Please," I plead with him, ignoring his secret jab. "I ... I, please don't tell Kal."

"Don't tell Kal what?" the man in question asks, stalking toward us like a man on a mission.

"That she's still in love with me," Stefan cockily taunts my husband.

"Yeah, I call bullshit on that." He looks to me. "What are you not telling me, babe?"

"I ... I ... I was sick again, Kal."

"Again?" he repeats, concern laces his one-word reply. He steps in front of me and rests his palm over my forehead, checking my temperature and being all swoony. "I really think you need to go to the doctor, you've been sick lots lately, baby, and I hate seeing you like this. You don't have a temperature, so that's a good thing."

"I'm fine," I tell him, sliding my arms around his waist for a cuddle.

"Maybe she's pregnant," Stefan unhelpfully adds. Looking over my shoulder at him, I glare and give him the evil eye. *Pucking douche*, I think to myself.

Kal pushes on my shoulders and grips my upper arms. "Are you?" he asks, staring intently at me.

My mouth opens and closes. I'm at a loss for what to say. I want to give him this as a Christmas present but I also know I'm a shitty liar and I don't want Kal thinking the worst of me. I'm so pucking screwed, looks like I'm going to have to ruin my Christmas surprise. However, before I can confess, Stefan begins to gag from behind me and then he rushes into the bathroom I just exited. From where we are standing, we can hear him dry heaving through the door.

"Maybe you both have food poisoning?" Kal voices before stepping over and knocking on the door. "You okay, Däuchmen?"

"Fine," he yells out before heaving again. Hearing him heaving sets me off and I race into the ladies' restroom, but I don't make it to the toilet, I throw up in the sink. A hand begins rubbing my back and I know it's Kal. "Kal," I whisper, "this is the ladies' restroom."

"I know, but my wife needs me." *Swoon*, how can my va-jay-jay swoon to life when I have vomit mouth? "And I'm not going anywhere."

"But your wife needs water, can you go get me some? Please?"

"Anything for you, baby." He places a kiss on the back of my head and leaves me to dry-heave in peace. Looks like my stomach is finally empty.

Kal returns a few moments later with water and Lexi. "Babe, I need to leave you with Lex. Doucheman and I have to do our thing now." He pauses and scrunches up his face. "I really hope he doesn't vomit on me."

"I'm sure you'll both be fine. I'll be out in a moment to watch you shine."

"You just look after you." He leans in for a kiss but I turn my head and vomit again, clearly my stomach wasn't empty after all. He pats my head and leaves me with Lexi. "Ugh, this better pass," I tell her.

"It will and if it helps, strong morning sickness is a sign of a healthy pregnancy."

"Doesn't really help, but I guess this ongo—" I don't get to finish because I throw up the water I just drank.

"I really think you need to tell your husband, he's so worried about you."

"I know, but it was going to be his Christmas present. Lex," I whine, "I don't know if I can wait 'til next week."

"So give him his present early," she suggests like the pucking genius she is.

My head snaps up and that light bulb clicks in my mind. "That's perfect, why didn't I think of that?"

"Probably 'cause your head is always in the toilet or you're stuffing your face with food. How it hasn't clicked, I will never know."

"Stefan guessed right away," I tell her, "And ... and I think he covered for me just now."

"Huh?" she questions as I stand up and lean against the sink.

"Just before, I ran into him after throwing up and he said, I was pregnant. Pretty sure it was a joke, but he knew from my facial expression that I am. I asked him not to tell Kal and then Kal arrived and he heard me say that. I was at a loss for what to say, but then Stefan started to fake vomit, well, I think it was fake."

Turning around, I wash my hands and think over what just happened. He was teasing me and then he was retching, did he just help me keep my secret? Or is he really sick? "Whatever the case, he just saved my ass."

"Let me get this straight, Stefan Däuchmen just helped you keep a secret?"

"Yep."

"Stefan Däuchmen didn't throw you under the bus?"

Slowly I nod. "Mmmhmpf."

"Are we in *The Twilight Zone*? 'Cause, what the puck?"

"I know, right? But whatever the case, I need to get out there so I can see my man shine, and then I'm going to give him his Christmas present early 'cause secrets and me aren't good." I nearly spilled the secret I know about her, but my brain kicked into gear and I kept my mouth shut. Look at me, I can keep a secret. We really must be in *The Twilight Zone* after all.

"Okay, let's do this." Lexi links arms with me and we head out of the bathroom.

Being up here with Stefan, I find myself in awe of the guy as I listen intently to his speech and that's something I never thought I would do. He's a douche, plain and simple, but as I sit here and take in his words, I realize he really put thought into this presentation. Now I kinda feel bad for ignoring most of his texts and calls this past week.

"... and with that being said, I'll wrap things up but before I do, I need to offer an apology." This piques my interest and I sit up straighter in my chair. "I need to apologize to my former teammates and coach. I really was a douche when I was playing here in New York. I thought my shit didn't stink and that the world owed me. I hurt a lot of people along the way. Sorry for not being the teammate and man I should have been, but I guess it worked out well for you, Kal, because you married a pretty great chick." He turns to face me. "Kallen, you're pretty great too, but your wife's better. I know we've had our differences, on and off the ice, but that's all in the past and I hope that one day we can become friends." Then he turns to Wren. "I also need to thank this amazing woman here last. Wren, thank you for keeping my ass in line and putting up with me, but most of all, Kallen and I need to thank you guys, our fans. Without fans we wouldn't have the desire to win like we do. You guys cheering us on is always the push we need to play at our best. Sure, some of you root for the wrong team." My teammates and I boo him. "And yes, I know I used to be a Crusher, but I'm now with the far superior team." His teammates cheer. "But rivalry is good when it's handled professionally and left on the ice. I think Kallen will agree with me, life is much simpler when we don't have management, or Wren, riding our butts."

"I don't know about Wren riding my butt 'cause, well, I'm not a douche, but I do have a wife and father-in-law who keep me in line."

"Yeah, boys and girls," Stefan singsongs, "don't

hook up with the coach's daughter because Coach will push you harder, on and off the ice."

"It's worth it if you ask me." Finding Chelsea at the back of the crowd, I blow her a kiss. She smiles and air kisses me back, but I notice an odd look on her face. She's here but she's not here, and that causes my worry for her to increase. Then I think about her throwing up all the time and her general offness lately, is she sick? Is she dying? What the puck is going on? What is she hiding from me?

JJ shouts, "You guys are whipped," from the back of the room, earning himself an elbow to the ribs from Lexi.

I realize I tuned out and missed the rest of Stefan's speech, but he's wrapping it up now, and I'm thankful for that because I need to be with my wife. "Life is hard," Stefan says, "we aren't always going to get along with everyone and that's okay, but we need to treat each other with respect. Life is difficult enough as it is, without making it harder for ourselves by focusing on the negatives." He pauses and looks to Wren, a look of contentment appears on his face. "A wise woman once told me to show respect to everyone, even those who don't deserve it because it reflects on you and your character in how you treat them." He then turns to me. "Jones, I'm sorry for being a jackass to you." He looks to the crowd and finds Chelsea. "And especially you, Chels. I let my insecurities fester and it wasn't until I was about to lose it all that I realized, I, and only I, can change what happens in my life."

"I ... ummm, wow, I don't know what to say."

"You don't have to say anything, just know, I'm sorry and I'm sure you'll make a great dad." My eyes widen at him mentioning kids and then he adds on, "One of these days."

"Thanks, man, and truth be told, I'm sorry too."

"What are you sorry for?"

"I'm not sure exactly but after your heartfelt speech, I felt like I needed to say it too. I'm sure I did just as many douchey things as you did."

"Let's leave the past in the past and focus on the future?" He offers me his hand and I take it, shaking it.

"I'd like that."

The crowd claps and when I look up, my eyes find my girl. I notice that she's wiping at her eyes as she starts to walk toward Stefan and me as we climb off the stage. "You guys, that was amazing," she says when we reach her.

"I meant it, Chels, I'm sorry. I was horrible to

you when we dated and the things I did to you, I'm ashamed of myself."

"As you said, it's in the past. I've moved on … and I think you might have too." I head nod toward Wren, who is talking with one of the organizers.

"I'm trying but she's stubborn."

"Is she worth the fight?" I ask him and before he even answers, I know what he's going to say.

He nods. "Yeah, she is."

"Then don't give up," Chels tells him. "Be the man I first fell in love with and she'll have no choice but to fall."

"How and why are you being so nice to me?"

"Because I'm happy and, Stefan, that's all I ever wanted for you. Sure, you and I didn't work out and you did the worst thing possible to a girl, but I never wanted you to be alone and unhappy. Everyone deserves happiness, Stefan, even douches who cheat."

"Thank you," he tells her. Chelsea then shocks him and wraps her arms around him, she whispers something to him and he nods, smiling at her when he pulls back. "And, Jones, thanks for today. It was eye-opening all around."

"It was. Thanks for making it fun because I was really dreading this."

"You and me both, but as it turns out, you're not so bad after all but just know, the next time we play you guys, I'm going to wipe the ice with your ass."

"And the douche is back," I tease him.

"Once a douche, always a douche," he replies nonchalantly. Waving us goodbye, he steps around us and walks over to Wren.

Turning to face Chelsea, I find her smiling, her eyes bright, something I haven't seen for a while now. "What are you smiling about, babe?"

"Nothing in particular but I have a surprise for you. Will ... will you come with me?"

"I'll go anywhere with you, Chelsea Jones. Any-pucking-where."

CHELSEA

Lacing my fingers through Kal's, we say our goodbyes to everyone and after pulling on our winter coats, we head out into the chilly December afternoon. We jump into a cab and leaning forward, I give the driver our home address. Kal looks at me inquisitively. "Just need to grab something from home quickly."

He nods and I can tell the suspense is killing him. It's not often I get to surprise him because, well, I suck with secrets and the fact I'm giving him this earlier than I planned confirms I can't keep my mouth shut. The driver pulls up and I climb out, quickly racing upstairs to grab the present for Kal, ever so thankful I already wrapped it.

With the gift safely tucked into my bag, I race back downstairs and ask the driver to take us to Rockefeller Center. "What are you up to, Mrs. Jones?"

"You'll find out soon, Mr. Jones."

Leaning into his side, I snuggle in and breathe him in. Nerves are starting to build and I feel like I could throw up again, but I swallow the lump down and concentrate on the gift in my bag. We finally pull up and Kal climbs out first before turning back to offer me his hand. "Such a gentleman," I coo as I take his hand and walk toward the tree. My heart rate increases the closer we get and my stomach begins to flutter with nerves and not the feeling to vomit—go me!

Arriving at the base of the tree, I tilt my head back and Kal wraps his arms around me from behind. Together we gaze up at the tree, enjoying the intimate moment.

"Ever since I watched *Home Alone* 2 when I was little with Kendall, I've loved this tree. I can't believe I've lived here for as long as I have and I've never been here before."

"Well, I'm glad to pop your tree viewing cherry." *And in a minute, I hope you love this spot for a whole new reason.* Taking a deep breath, I spin in his arms to face him. "Merry Christmas, husband," I whisper and hold out the narrow gift box.

"Christmas isn't 'til next week."

"I know, but I want you to have this now." He stares at the box, then at me and then back at the box again. "Open it," I encourage him. He tugs at the bow on the top and is struggling to get it undone. I shake my head and laugh, covering his hand, he looks at me. "It's a gift box, you just lift the lid."

"Ohh, oops." He shrugs and then proceeds to remove the lid. He stares down at the positive pregnancy test and then lifts his gaze to mine. "You gave me a pregnancy test." Nodding, I wait for him to register that it's positive, but his face remains neutral. He lifts it up and that's when I realize it's upside down, the pink positive sign is facing me, he's looking at the plain white plastic side. Reaching up, I spin it over so he can see the positive sign. He stares at it for a few beats and then his eyes widen. "Are we? Are you?"

Nodding, my grin widens. "Yep, we, well, I am."

"Are you pucking with me?"

Shaking my head from side to side, I reach up and cup his cheek. "I'm not pucking with you, Kal, I'm pregnant."

"With a baby?" I laugh, it's scary how much alike he and Margot are.

"Yes, with a baby. Your baby."

"Are you serious?"

"Mmmhmpf," I reply with a nod. He just stares at me, his expression neutral and I can't tell if he's excited, angry, or what, but then the biggest of big Kallen Jones smiles appears on his face and all my worries flutter away with the snowflakes that just started to fall. It snowing right now makes this moment perfect in every way.

"This is the best pucking present ever, Chels, and it explains why you've been so sick."

"Pretty much."

"Why didn't you tell me as soon as you found out?"

"'Cause you were in jail and I wanted to give you an amazing Christmas present to end the year on a high."

"Best present ever, and I'm definitely ending the year on a high."

"Merry Christmas, Kal."

"Merry Christmas, Chels." He scoops me into his arms and spins us around. "I'm gonna be a dad!" he shouts into the air. Placing me back on my feet, he stares into my eyes. "I pucking love you."

"I pucking love you too, now take me home and ravage me."

"With pucking pleasure." He dips me backward and presses his lips to mine for a kiss that leaves me breathless, before he whisks me home and we have a pucking good night, naked and sweaty between the sheets. Kal can play my body with precision. He knows exactly where to press, where to suck, and he pucks like there's no tomorrow.

I'm the luckiest gal in the world.

This is gearing up to be a pucking good Christmas.

KALLEN

"So are we going to tell your mom and dad at brunch this morning?"

"Well, Mom already knows—"

"What? How?"

"Well, the night you and Stefan got arrested and Mom was here with me, I threw up when she made me a coffee. She did the same when she was pregnant with me. She ducked out, grabbed a test, and one lil' pee later, it was confirmed."

"Ohh, right," I reply with a nod, hating that while I was in jail for brawling, my wife was alone when she found out she was pregnant. "So, we'll tell your dad today?"

"Yep. Are you scared?"

"Well, I wasn't 'til you said that."

"Are you scared he's going to kick your ass for defiling his Pumpkin and knocking her up?"

"Puck yes, I am, he's scary when it comes to you."

"Who knew the big bad goalie for the New York Crushers is scared of his coach and father-in-law?"

"We can't all be perfect like you," I tell my amazing wife. "Now, if you don't go and put some clothes on we're going to be late. 'Cause, babe, you are sexy in lingerie at the best of times but when you're pregnant and glowing in lingerie, you're pucking phenomenal."

She stalks over to me and I'm rooted to the spot, trapped in her seductive web. She traces her finger down my chest and toys with the knot in my towel. "You like what you see, baby?" she breathlessly whispers before dropping to her knees and removing my towel. "'Cause I definitely like what I see and I think he's happy to see me too." She places a kiss on the tip of my dick before opening her mouth and sliding her lips down my shaft. Raking her teeth gently on the way back up.

"Puck me," I groan as her head bobs up and down. Sliding my fingers into her hair, I grip her head and guide her back and forth. The tip hitting the back of her throat causes her to make that gagging sound that turns me the puck on. She reaches up and cups my balls and it's game over for me. With a guttural grunt, I come down her throat. She sucks every last drop from me. My dick pops out of her mouth and she wipes at the corners of her lips before sucking on her finger. I may have just come, but the carnal look on her face has my dick springing back to life.

"Your turn," I inform her, but she shakes her head.

"Later, because we'll be late if that tongue of yours touches my body." She stands up and turns to get dressed.

Reaching out, I grab her wrist and pull her back to me. Hugging her from behind, I lean forward and whisper, "Then we're going to be late because I need to fuck you with my tongue now." Spinning her around, I drop to my knees, throw her leg over my shoulder, and I kiss her through her panties.

"Kal," she moans, rocking herself against my face.

"Yes, wife?"

"Hurry up, I need you now."

"As you wish." Moving her panties to the side, I spear my tongue deep inside her. She grips the sides of my head and shoves me into her, grinding herself on my tongue and chin. Sucking on her clit, she moans in a guttural way that has my cock coming back to life. I need to fuck her and I need to do it now.

Pulling away from her, she whines in protest as I drop to my ass. Gripping her hips, I tear her panties off her body and guide her down onto my cock. The head slides between her folds and the two of us groan in delight as she sinks down to the hilt. She grips my shoulders and begins to ride me like a bucking bronco. "Yes," she pants as I meet her thrust for thrust. "Harder," she demands as she slams herself down on me.

Chelsea has always been a sweet lover but seeing her lose control like this is out of this world amazing. She throws her head back and howls as she crashes over the edge. Seeing her lose control sets me off, and together we draw out our climax, milking every last drop from each other's body.

She collapses onto my chest and I wrap my arms around her. "We're definitely gonna be late now." She giggles into my chest. "We can blame morning sickness," I reply into her hair, causing her to lift up and slap my chest.

"We cannot blame our baby for what just happened."

"Milk it while you can," I say.

She slaps my chest again. "Kallen Jones, that's terrible ... but depending on Daddy's anger, it can be our backup plan."

"Deal, now we better get moving, otherwise, we'll be really late ... much like the first brunch with them."

Thirty minutes later and only ten minutes late, Chelsea and I walk hand in hand into the diner and over to Coach and Nessa. "Morning," I singsong as I slide into the booth. Chels joins me after kissing her mom and dad hello. Slinging my arm over her shoulder, I pull her to my side and kiss her temple. It feels like since she told me she's pregnant, I've fallen in love with her all over again, but in a more intense way.

"You two ever going to get out of the honeymoon phase?" Coach asks, hailing the waitress and ordering four coffees.

"Just tea for me," Chels says, and then she looks to her dad. "And you are one to talk, you two are still all lovey-dovey and you've been married for eleventy billion years."

"Ease up there, Pumpkin, I'm not that old."

"Yeah, you are, Grandpa," I tease, earning myself

a whack in the stomach from Chels and a glare from Coach.

"Speaking of Grandpa," Chels says, taking a deep breath, "you're going to be one."

All eyes are on Coach as we await his reaction. He doesn't utter a word. Just sits there rapidly blinking. No one breathes, we all wait for him to make the first move. "Did you just say I'm going to be a grandpa?"

"Yes, Daddy. You're going to be a grandpa and Mom's going to be Nanny Ness."

His gaze snaps to mine. "You knocked my daughter up?"

"Dad," Chels complains.

"David," Nessa berates him with a slap to the arm.

"Yep," I timidly reply with a head nod.

Again, silence falls over the table. The waitress appears. "What can I get ya?" She's oblivious to the silence right now.

"Can we have a few more moments?" Nessa politely says to the waitress.

"Sure, whatevs," she nonchalantly replies, moving on to the next booth.

"Say something, Daddy," Chelsea says after the waitress leaves.

"I'm gonna be a grandpa."

"Yep," I reply and just when I think he's going to yell at me, a smile graces his face.

"I'm gonna be a grandpa." He turns to Nessa. "We're gonna be grandparents." He excitedly voices, "Chelsea has a baby in her tummy. My baby's having a baby." He slaps the table, causing the cutlery to clatter around. "My baby's having a baby," he repeats as he slides out of the booth and pulls Chels up into his arms. "So pucking happy," he murmurs into her hair.

Nessa and I sit here grinning as we watch Chelsea and her dad embrace. He grips her head in his palms and places a kiss on her temple. Then he turns his attention to me. "You hurt either one of them, I hurt you."

"Understood, sir," I reply with a nod, slightly shitting myself at his warning. He didn't go this daddy bear when I asked him permission to marry Chels.

"Good." He nods and then looks to Chels, who is still standing, tears welling in her eyes. "You okay, Pumpkin?"

"Perfectly happy," she cries as a tear cascades down her cheek. "My hormones are hormoning and I'm starving."

"As luck would have it, babe, we are in a diner, so sit down and we can order."

Chelsea drops down beside me and when the waitress returns, she orders what feels like one of everything off the menu. When my baby momma is full, we exit the diner and begin walking down Broadway. "So, when's your first ultrasound?" Nessa asks, just as a deep voice shouts, "You're pregnant?"

We all turn toward the W Hotel and see Stefan and a sheepish-looking Wren staring at us. "I ... umm, yeah, I am," Chels replies, not sure if she should be confirming the news, especially to him. I know yesterday we kinda mended fences and all that, but it's not like we're buddy buddy and he'd be the first person I'd want to know.

He smiles. "Guessed it," Stefan cockily replies. "Seems you're not a very good goalie after all, you let one slip past the goal ... but then again, in this instance, I think you want to miss, right?"

"Stefan," Wren berates him. "Don't be so rude and crass over something so exciting. Congratulations to you both," she offers with a smile to Chels and me.

"Thanks, it was a shock but we're happy," I tell them.

A silence envelops us but the moment is interrupted when a kid comes up to us. "Mr. Jones, Mr. Däuchmen, can ... can I get your autographs?"

"Of course," I tell the kid and I drop down to a knee so we're the same height. Chels hands me a pen and I sign the card in the kid's hands. I notice it's a birthday card. "Is it your birthday today?"

He nods and grins. "Yep, I'm ten today."

"Well, happy birthday, lil' man." I ruffle his hair and then Stefan takes the pen and card from me and signs it.

"Can I get a pic too, please?"

"Sure," Stefan says.

Stefan and I pose with the boy while Chelsea chats to his parents. "She's pretty," he whispers to me.

"The prettiest," I agree.

"One day I want to play hockey like you and I'm going to have an even prettier girlfriend."

"You do that, and I'll be in the stands cheering you on." He races over to his mom and excitedly tells her what I just said. Chels looks over and I throw a wink at her. She blushes and it reminds me of her cheeks from earlier this morning when she was riding me. My cock begins to twitch and I have to think of a naked Doucheman to deflate him.

"You really are going to be a great dad," Stefan says, his words shocking me.

"Thanks, man ... you will too ... one day."

He laughs. "One day, but not anytime soon. I still need to work on me first."

"Well, you're doing a good job, keep at it."

"Thanks, Jones."

"You're welcome, Däuchmen." With that, we say our goodbyes and I whisk my wife home for an afternoon on the sofa, eating ice cream and binge-watching *Stranger Things*.

Chelsea is sound asleep in my arms when there's a knock at the door. Sliding out from under her, I answer to find Phil, the doorman, standing there with a gift box. "Delivery for you, sir."

"Thanks, Phil."

I take the gift and head back inside, placing it on the island counter. I lift the lid and inside is a mini hockey stick and a onesie. Lifting it up, I read the front and it says, 'Future LA Legends player.' "Get pucked," I mumble as I notice a card. Pulling it out, I read.

Congrats to you both!
Thought I'd get the lil' man a gift, hope he
loves it as much as I do.
Let's go Legends.

"That pucking douche," I growl.

"Who's a pucking douche?"

"Who else, look what that puckhead got the baby." I hold the onesie up and show Chels, she begins to cackle.

"Ohh, I love it," she says. She picks up the hockey stick and turns it to face me, it has 'BABY JONES' etched into it.

"That's cute," I tell her, "but our baby is not wearing that shit." I toss the onesie to the side.

"Don't be a douche," she teases me. "We just got rid of one, we don't need another."

"Fine," I huff. "But how does he know it's a boy?"

"He's just guessing, time will tell. Now, come snooze with me, Momma is still tired."

Sweeping her up into my arms, I whisk her into our bedroom and we have a snooze ... after we get our puck on.

CHELSEA

... Christmas morning

Lying in bed, I keep my eyes closed, willing the sickness away. Cracking open my eyelid, I let out a breath and smile when I don't feel the need to vomit. Slowly, I sit up and from the corner of my eye, I see a packet of saltines on the side table and a glass of water. My husband is the best.

Grabbing a cracker, I nibble on it and then I hear the banging that woke me again. With cracker in hand, I slip my feet into my slippers and follow the noises down the hallway, but I notice the door to the spare room is slightly ajar. "Kal," I call out as I push on the door.

The door swings open and my eyes widen at what I see before me. Our spare room is no longer a spare room, it's the most amazing nursery I have ever seen. The walls have been painted light gray and along the center of the back wall is the most gorgeous glossy, white wooden crib, which is decked out in Crushers blankets, complete with hockey-themed mobile. On the wall next to the crib is a hockey stick art piece that I can see a rocker chair in front of. On the opposite wall is a Canadian, a US, and a Crushers flag and there are many more cardboard boxes.

This is not what I envisioned my child's nursery to look like but now that I've seen this, it's perfect. My eyes well with tears and when a set of muscular arms slide around me, I smile. Kal leans in and nuzzles into my neck. "You like?"

Spinning around to face him, I gaze up at my sexier-than-puck husband and nod. "It's perfect, Kal."

"I was hoping to have it finished before you woke up as a Christmas surprise, but that pucking stick thing took forever to make."

"You made that?" I ask him.

"Yep, with my bare hands." Those hands are currently squeezing the peachy globes of my ass.

"Merry Christmas, babe." He drops to his knees and whispers to my belly, "Merry Christmas, Bug." Kal and I chose to call the baby Bug while we wait to find out if we're having a boy or girl. The thought of referring to him or her as 'It' just didn't sit right, and since we thought I had a bug, Bug seemed like the perfect name.

He stands back up and wraps his arms around me again. "Merry Christmas, Kal," I whisper, lifting to my toes to press my lips to his for a kiss. A bang on the front door pulls us apart. "Who would be here at eight on Christmas morning?"

He shrugs at me. "Guess we better answer it and find out." His response is cryptic and I wonder if he knows something I don't, but he looks just as clueless as me right now. Pulling out of his embrace, I pad down the hallway toward the front door when they impatiently bang on the door again. "Coming," I mumble. When I swing the door open, I come face-to-face with a huge pile of Christmas presents that has legs and two hands.

"Hello?" I question by way of greeting.

"Pumpkin," my dad says from behind the pile. "Grandpa needs you to let him in. Please?" Yes, in the few days since Dad found out, he's been referring to himself as Grandpa ... and in third person. It was funny to begin with but now, it's just annoying.

"Nah," I tease, "I'm just gonna stand here in the doorway all day and stare at this massive pile of presents with hands and legs that talks."

"Pumpkin," he warns, and as he growls, a present from the top topples to his feet. "Shit," he hisses, "I hope that wasn't one of the breakable ones."

"What the puck?" Kal says, joining us.

"Dad went overboard with presents."

"Grandpa did not."

"I see we're still on the third person thing," Kal states with an eye roll, all of us sick of the third personing.

"Mmmhmpf." I nod.

"Kallen Jones," Dad growls, "if you don't let me in, I'll bench you for the rest of the season."

"Like you'd let your star goalie warm the bench," I scoff, "but in the spirit of Christmas, come on in, Dad."

"Grandpa thanks you, Pumpkin," he says, somehow shuffling through the doorway and not dropping any more presents.

Bending down, I pick up the dropped one and look into the hallway for Mom. "Where's Mom?"

"At home sleeping, she looked so peaceful and I didn't want to wake her."

"You left Mom at home to wake alone on Christmas morning?"

"Well, yeah, I had to drop off the presents for Cletus the Fetus."

"You did not just refer to my baby as Cletus the Fetus, did you, Dad?"

"Grandpa did because saying It felt too impersonal."

"And Cletus the Fetus is personal?"

"Well, what should Grandpa call him then?"

"SHE," I emphasize that word, "is being referred to as Bug."

"Bug, Grandpa likes that," Dad says as my phone begins to ring. Walking over to the kitchen island, I smile when I see Mom's face. "Merry Christmas, Mom."

"Merry Christmas, honey, is that husband of mine there?"

"Yes, Grandpa is here and he has the whole of Toys R Us with him. Why did you let him go crazy?"

"Try stopping that man, ever since your ultrasound, he's been telling everyone." I had my first ultrasound two days ago, turns out, I'm twelve weeks along. Remember that mini freak-out back in October, yeah, well, I was pregnant then. The test I took after the Crushers lost to LA was a false negative because it was only early days. It seems that I conceived on our honeymoon. Since Kal is a celebrity, when we were seen coming out of the doctor's clinic, within minutes, the whole world knew too. That night we were all over the entertainment channels. The joys of being married to a pro player. "Give me ten minutes and I'll head over."

"Take your time, Mom, we'll be here when you get here."

"Love you, Chels."

"You too, Mom." Hanging up, I turn around and my eyes widen when I see all the presents laid out, when there's another knock at the door. "I'll get it." Shuffling over, I open it and once again, I come face-to-face with a pile of presents. "Dad, what the puck?"

"Phil, thanks for your help," Dad says to our present-laden doorman, ignoring me. He ushers Phil in and helps him unload the presents.

"Merry Christmas, Chelsea and Kallen," Phil says with a nod before exiting our apartment.

"Dad, this is too much."

"Never. Grandpa is going to spoil Bug and it all starts with her first Christmas."

"You do realize that right now, she's the size of a plum?" *Ohh plum, I could go for a plum right now* I think to myself as I stare at Dad, who is placing a hockey puck under the tree. "Daaaaaad, she won't need that 'til she's—"

"Born," Kallen interrupts. "Need to start on the next generation of Jones hockey players."

"Puck me." I rub my stomach. "Bug, I'm so sorry that your family is crazy."

"Grandpa heard that, Pumpkin," Dad says as he walks into the kitchen and over to the coffee maker. He sets about making coffee for everyone, and a tea for me, while Kal starts arranging a fruit platter. Walking over to him, I pinch a strawberry off the plate and take a bite. Closing my eyes, I moan as the sweet juices explode and dance on my tongue.

Opening my eyes, I see Kal staring at me, a heated look is reflecting back at me, and suddenly I'm no longer thinking about plums. I'm thinking about my husband and all the sexy things I want to do to him on the kitchen island. He and I screw on this counter more than we eat at it, which is probably a good thing for sanitary purposes.

Thankfully, there's a knock at the door and it bursts the connection because we cannot do that on the counter right now, not with Dad currently arguing with the coffee maker. "I'll get it," I say again.

This time, when I open the door, it's Mom, with no presents. "What, no presents?" I tease. "The last two people to arrive were laden with presents."

"Sorry to disappoint, sweetheart, but I can offer you and Bug a hug?"

"Bug and I would love that." Mom envelops me in a hug and I embrace her back just as tightly. "Merry Christmas, Mom."

"Merry Christmas, baby girl." She pulls back and stares at me, she's smiling brightly and I find myself grinning back at her. Linking my arm with Mom's, we walk into the apartment and her eyes widen when she sees all the gifts. "I'd like to state, I had no part in this present explosion."

"No, but you did go crazy on Baby Barn ordering clothes," Dad informs us, trying to show that Mom is just as baby crazy as he is.

"I'm a nanny, it's my prerogative to spoil my grandbaby with clothes."

"And it's my prerogative to spoil my grandbaby with anything I want," Dad throws back at her.

"We've created grandmonsters," Kal whispers as he wraps his arms around me from behind, resting his hands on my tiny baby belly.

Our first Christmas as a married couple started off rocky, thanks to a rivalry on the ice that threatened to derail Christmas with an arrest. But now, the air is clear, paving the way for a bright future, on and off the ice. The rivalry between Kal and Stefan is finally over, something Bug and I are extremely happy for.

As I stand here in my husband's arms and watch my parents bicker about the arrival of their grandbaby, I realize that it's a pucking good Christmas and next year is going to be so pucking great.

THE PUCKING END!

PLAYLIST

Mr. Jones - Counting Crows
Bad Day - Daniel Powter
Let in Snow! - Michael Bublé
Merry Christmas - Ed Sheehan, Elton John
Santa Claus is Coming to Town - Kylie Minogue,
Frank Sinatra
I Knew I Loved You - Savage Garden
Fight Song - Rachel Platten
I'll Be There For You - The Rembrants
Use Somebody - Kings of Leon
Meant to Be - Bebe Rexha feat. Florida Georgia Line
Flashlight - Jessie J
Halo - Beyoncé
Just Give Me a Reason - P!nk feat. Nate Reuss
Story of My Life - One Direction

Say Something - A Great Big World, Christina
Aguilera
Unconditionally - Katy Perry
Everything Has Changed - Taylor Swift, Ed
Sheehan
Tequila - Dan + Shay

This playlist can be found on Spotify.

Want to know more about how Kallen and Chelsea fell in love? You can in I Pucking Hate That I Love You.

I vowed I'd never give my heart to another hockey player again. I learned my lesson the first time. But then I met Kallen Jones and he became a huge problem.

Not only is he on my "Don't Fall in Love with A Hockey Player" list, but he's also sitting pretty high on my "I want you" list. But I can't date a puckhead again.

It doesn't matter how good looking he is with his blue eyes, lickable abs, and heart of gold. He's a hockey player and my dad is his coach. Except Kallen isn't like the others. He treats me like a princess and has me doubting my decision and breaking my vow at every turn.

Until he turns out to be just like the last puckhead I gave my heart to.

I pucking hate him but I also pucking love him…I'm so pucking screwed.

ACKNOWLEDGMENTS

These things never get any easier and I always feel like I've forgotten someone so this is a blanket thank you to everyone who I have crossed paths with on this authoring journey.

Karen Hrdlicka from **Barren Acres Editing**; thank you for everything that you do for me.

Lisa; thank you for checking all my I's are dotted, my T's are crossed and there's no extra e's or s's.

Kirsty from **Vanilla Lily**; thank you for this alternate cover, as soon as I saw the set, I had to have them. I cannot wait to see they babies in print.

Lainey from **DS Promotions** and all the bloggers, thank you for helping me share A Pucking Good Christmas with the world. Without your support us authors wouldn't be where we are. You guys pucking rock!

My beta babes **Bec, Tara, Sarah, and Vi;** I would be lost without you ladies. You give me advice when I second guess everything and you helped to bring this story to life. Thank you from the bottom of my heart.

Troy, my husband, my everything. You really are awesome at what you do and you're an even better husband and father. Love you long-time dude.

To my munchkins, **Piper** and **Kade**. You two are my greatest achievement and I'm so lucky to have you both in my life. Love you long-time guys and I look forward to the day when you are forty and can finally read my books.

And finally, **you, my reader**. This book is a different genre for me but I have to say, its one of my favs and I hope that you loved Chelsea and Kallen as much as I do.

Cheers,

Dana XoXoX

ALSO BY DL GALLIE

STAND ALONES

Antecedent

Doc Steel

Oops

Off the Books

Fractured:A driven world novel

Deck...the Balls

Secrets and Sunrises

Always in the Cards

Out of Nowhere

Before the Ashes

After the Ashes

Love Me Like You Do

Never Let Me Go

Seven Nights

Seven Kisses

PUCKING NOVELS

I Pucking Hate That I Love You

A Pucking Good Christmas

It's Pucking Fake (appearing in Fake It Till You Make It)

I Pucking Hate That You Love Me

...and a few pucking more

FALLING NOVELS

These men make it hard not to fall for them

Falling for Dr. Kelly

Falling for Dr. Knight

Falling for Agent Cox

Falling for Agent Cruz

LORDS OF CRESTWOOD PREP

Co-write with Tara Lee

Thatcher

Reign

Hendrix

Saint

THE UNEXPECTED SERIES

When it comes to love, expect the unexpected

The Unexpected Gift

The Unexpected Letter

The Unexpected Package

The Unexpected Connection

The Unexpected series: The Complete Collection

THE CASTAWAY GROVE COLLECTION

Love has arrived in the Grove

Oasis

Unequivocal Love

Five Words

Broken Rules

...and a few more to come.

The Castaway Grove Collection, Vol 1

THE LIQUOR CABINET SERIES

Liquor has never been so disturbingly saucy

Malt Me (Book 1)

Tequila Healing (Book 2)

Wine Not (Book 3)

The Final Shot (Book 4)

The Liquor Cabinet: Series boxset

All of these books are available on Amazon.

FACEBOOK ~ INSTAGRAM ~ BOOKBUB

GOODREADS ~ WEBSITE

dlgallieauthor@outlook.com

Sign up to my newsletter

ABOUT THE AUTHOR

DL Gallie is from Queens-
land, Australia, but she's
lived in many different
places all over the world,
including the UK and
Canada. She currently
resides in Central Queens-

land with her husband and two munchkins. She and
her husband have been together since she was
sixteen, and although they drive each other crazy at
times, she couldn't imagine her life without him.

Shortly after her son was born, DL began reading
again. With encouragement from her husband, she
picked up the pen and started writing, and now the
voices in her head won't shut up.

DL enjoys listening to music, drinking white wine in
the summer, red wine in the winter, and beer all year

round. She's also never been known to turn down a cocktail, especially a margarita.